BAKUGAN
BATTLE BRAWLERS

READY TO BRAWL
BEST BATTLES
GUIDEBOOK

By Tracey West

SCHOLASTIC INC.

New York   Toronto   London   Auckland
Sydney   Mexico City   New Delhi   Hong Kong

ISBN-13: 978-0-545-15519-9
ISBN-10: 0-545-15519-3

Published by Scholastic Inc. SCHOLASTIC and
associated logos are trademarks and/or registered
trademarks of Scholastic Inc.

12 11 10 9 8 7 6 5 4 3 2 1   9 10 11 12 13 14/0

Cover art by Carlo LoRaso
Printed in the U.S.A.
First printing, September 2009

LET'S BRAWL!

Ever since Dan Kuso and his friends invented the Bakugan game, brawlers have been facing each other in heated battles. Different players use different strategies to try to come out on top. Some memorize every rule of the game. Some players use Ability Cards. And others just toss out their Bakugan— and hope they get lucky.

Dan and his friends have their own unique styles on the field. In this guide, you'll read about some of the most exciting Bakugan battles so far. You'll see some of the mad moves skilled players use to win. And in the middle of the book, you'll learn about some of the best cards to have in your deck.

THE MASKED BRAWLER

Runo was the first of Dan's friends to lose her Bakugan to mysterious Masquerade. Dan got angry that somebody out there was sending Bakugan to the Doom Dimension. He issued a challenge on the web—and Masquerade answered.

It was the first time Dan and Masquerade battled, and the masked brawler dominated the brawl. He sent two of Dan's Bakugan to the Doom Dimension—and Dan almost lost Drago, too.

Move 1

The battle begins as Masquerade and Dan each throw out a Gate Card. Dan throws his Pyrus Serpenoid onto the field.

Move 2

Masquerade throws Darkus Reaper onto the Gate Card with Serpenoid. With 370 Gs, Reaper has more power than Serpenoid.

370
320

Move 3

Dan turns over his Gate Card. The card gives a huge boost to Pyrus Bakugan—300 Gs. Dan gets ready to take down Reaper.

620

Move 4

But Masquerade has an Ability Card up his sleeve. Dimension Four wipes out the effect of Dan's Gate Card. Serpenoid loses the power boost, and Reaper wins the round.

370

RUNO'S REVENGE

Masquerade sent a brawler named Tatsuya to battle Dan—but Runo intercepted the message. After losing her Bakugan to Masquerade, she wanted revenge.

Runo and Tatsuya faced off down by the river. Tatsuya started out strong with his Pyrus Garganoid, but Runo found a way to defeat it. In the end, her Tigrerra helped her win the brawl.

Move 1

After Pyrus Garganoid took down Runo's Juggernoid, there is one Gate Card left on the field. Runo throws out a Haos Saurus to stand on the card.

280

Move 2

Tatsuya sends out his Pyrus Garganoid again. The beast has 330 Gs, and gets even stronger when Tatsuya uses an Ability Card called Fire Judge. Saurus looks like he doesn't stand a chance.

440
280

Move 3

Runo uses an Ability Card to counteract the effects of Tatsuya's Ability Card. Garganoid falls back down to 330 Gs—but that's still enough to beat Saurus. Or is it?

330
280

Move 4

Tatsuya attacks with Garganoid, but Runo has one more move she can make. She turns over the Gate Card. The special card allows Saurus to increase its Gs to match the most powerful Bakugan Runo has. Now Saurus has 340 Gs—and Garganoid is defeated.

330
340

CONFIDENCE IS KEY

Alice met a young brawler named Christopher who was about to give up on Bakugan. An older brawler named Travis kept beating him in battle.

When Travis challenged Christopher again, Alice coached Travis from the sidelines. In the end, Chris couldn't hear Alice, and had to win the battle on his own. Thanks to a boost of confidence, he powered up his Aquos Juggernoid to take down the rest of Travis's Bakugan.

Move 1

Christopher only has one Bakugan left—Juggernoid. Travis throws Darkus Mantris onto the card with Juggernoid. Darkus Mantris has 340 Gs. Juggernoid has 330.

340 330

Move 2

Travis uses an Ability Card, Slice Cutter, to reduce Juggernoid's Gs by 50.

340 280

Move 3

Christopher uses his own Ability Card, Depth Tornado. The card increases Juggernoid's power to 380 Gs. Juggernoid attacks Mantris and wins the round.

340 380

A SLEW OF SURPRISES

Marucho couldn't believe it when pop stars Jenny and Jewls showed up at his mansion. Then the divas challenged him and Dan to a brawl. The boys accepted—and were shocked when the girls showed they each had a Doom Card. They were working for Masquerade!

Jenny and Jewls turned out to be skilled brawlers. They combined diagonal aspects of their attributes to make some killer moves. But the biggest surprise in the brawl had to be when Marucho used Aquos Preyas for the first time. The Bakugan revealed he had the special ability to change attributes.

Move 1

Jewls tosses Subterra Stinglash onto the Gate Card she put down. Marucho knows that when she turns the Gate Card over, Stinglash will probably get a big power boost.

290

Move 2

Aquos Preyas urges Marucho to send him out. Marucho agrees, and Preyas stands on the card with Stinglash.

290 300

Move 3

Preyas has more Gs than Stinglash—but Jewls is confident that when she turns over the Gate Card, her Stinglash will win. But Preyas quickly changes his attribute to Subterra.

290 300

Move 4

The Gate Card turns over. It gives Subterra Bakugan a boost of 150 Gs. Since Preyas is now Subterra, he gets the boost, too. Preyas attacks Stinglash and wins the round.

440 450

USE THESE CARDS!

These Bakugan cards can help you win a brawl—
if you know how to use them.

GATE CARDS

CARD FORCE

The G-Power Gate bonus is raised by 50 for each Ability Card in a used pile when this Gate Card is revealed.

TIP: Use this card late in the brawl, when you have a few Ability Cards in your used pile. Then rack up the points.

DUCK & WIN

The Bakugan with the lowest G power wins this battle.

TIP: Stand your Bakugan on this Gate Card if you know your opponent has more powerful Bakugan than you do.

STAND OFF

No Ability Cards may be played in this battle.

TIP: Use this if your Bakugan has more Gs than your opponent, and you think your opponent will use an Ability Card to win.

G-POWER EXCHANGE

The Bakugan have their printed G power swapped.

TIP: Make sure to use this only if your Bakugan has low G power.

ABILITY CARDS

DAN'S THROW

Play before you roll. If this roll results in a battle, you may take back one of your Ability Cards from your used pile.

Joue avant de lancer. S'il y a bataille lors de cette manche, tu pourras reprendre une de tes cartes Capacités de la pile "Hors Jeu".

BA162-AB-SM "Bakugan" 2008 Spin Master LTD. & SEGA Toys . 30/48.

JULIE'S THROW

Play before you roll. Pick an enemy Bakugan™ on a Gate Card. Your opponent puts that Bakugan™ in his used pile and replaces it with one of his unused Bakugan™.

Joue avant de lancer. Choisis un Bakugan™ ennemi sur une carte Portail. Ton adversaire place ce Bakugan™ dans sa pile "Hors Jeu" et le remplace par un de ses Bakugan™ inutilisés.

BA150-AB-SM "Bakugan" 2008 Spin Master LTD. & SEGA Toys . 28/48.

SHUN'S THROW

Play before you roll. Look at one face down Gate card in the arena.

Joue avant de lancer. Regarde une des cartes Portail de l'arène.

BA160-AB-SM "Bakugan" 2008 Spin Master LTD. & SEGA Toys . 28/48.

RUNO'S THROW

Play before you roll. You may roll a Bakugan™ from your used pile this turn (you still only roll one Bakugan™ this turn).

Joue avant de lancer. Tu peux lancer un Bakugan™ de ta pile "Hors Jeu" lors de ce tour (attention, tu ne peux jouer qu'un seul Bakugan™ pendant ce tour).

BA159-AB-SM "Bakugan" 2008 Spin Master LTD. & SEGA Toys . 27/48.

DAN'S THROW

Play before you roll. If this roll results in a battle, you may take back one of your Ability Cards from your used pile.

TIP: Use this after you use your best Ability Card to get it back.

JULIE'S THROW

Play before you roll. Pick an enemy Bakugan on a Gate Card. Your opponent puts that Bakugan in his used pile and replaces it with one of his unused Bakugan.

TIP: Save this for the end of the battle, when your opponent hopes to wipe you out with one powerful move.

SHUN'S THROW

Play before you roll. Look at one facedown Gate Card in the arena.

TIP: Use this to see what move your opponent is planning.

RUNO'S THROW

Play before you roll. You may roll a Bakugan from your used pile this turn.

TIP: Does your opponent have his most powerful Bakugan on the field? Have you already used yours? Use this card to bring it back into action.

SHUN'S BIG SAVE

When the battle between Dan and Masquerade heated up, they tried to recruit brawlers to help them out. Both Dan and Masquerade approached Shun, the number-one ranked brawler.

Shun didn't want to take sides. He and Dan and Masquerade began a three-way battle. Masquerade hoped Shun would team up with him to defeat Dan. But in a stunning move, Shun sacrificed his Monarus to save Dan's Drago. Shun had chosen a side after all—the right one.

Move 1

Masquerade has Darkus Laserman and Darkus Reaper on the field. Dan's Drago is on a Gate Card with Reaper, ready to battle. Now it's Shun's turn to throw—and he has Monarus stand on a Gate Card.

Move 2

Masquerade uses an Ability Card, Third Judgment. This allows him to bring another Darkus Bakugan onto the Gate Card so the two can combine their G Powers. Masquerade chooses his powerful Hydranoid.

Move 3

Dan tries an Ability Card, Boosted Dragon, to give Drago extra power. But it's not enough to take down Hydranoid and Reaper combined.

Move 4

It looks like Drago is toast—but then Shun makes his surprise move. He uses the Ability Card Crimson Twister to move Drago to the Gate Card with Monarus. He orders Monarus to attack, knowing his Bakugan will lose. But Drago is safe—and Masquerade's plan has failed, for now.

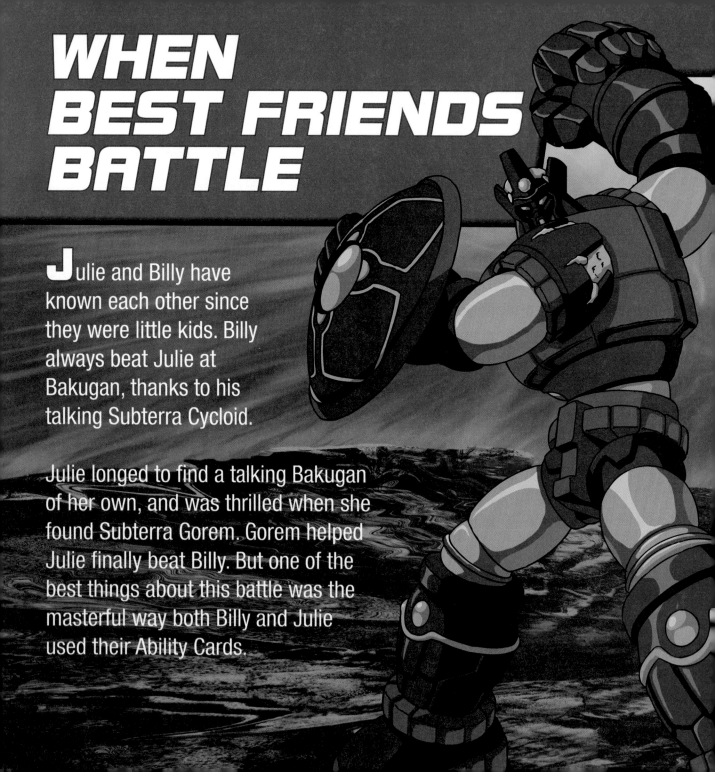

WHEN BEST FRIENDS BATTLE

Julie and Billy have known each other since they were little kids. Billy always beat Julie at Bakugan, thanks to his talking Subterra Cycloid.

Julie longed to find a talking Bakugan of her own, and was thrilled when she found Subterra Gorem. Gorem helped Julie finally beat Billy. But one of the best things about this battle was the masterful way both Billy and Julie used their Ability Cards.

Move 1

In the middle of the battle, there are two Game Cards on the field, and Billy's Subterra Cycloid stands on one of them. Billy uses Stare Down, which means that any Bakugan who stands where a Gate Card has already been thrown will lose 50 Gs. Julie avoids this trap by throwing her Gate Card out of range and standing Subterra Manion on it.

370

300

Move 2

Billy uses the Ability Card Grand Slide to move Manion's Gate Card next to Cycloid. Manion drops 50 Gs, and Cycloid is able to attack. Cycloid wins the round.

370

250

Move 3

Julie throws Subterra Gorem, who stands on the Gate Card with Cycloid. She uses the Ability Card Mega Impact to increase Gorem's Gs by 50.

370

430 250

Move 4

Billy opens the Gate Card, and Gorem's Gs drop down 100 Gs to 330. But Julie's Mega Impact is still in effect. Before Cycloid can attack, his points drop by 100, too. Gorem has more Gs and wins the round.

270

330 250

CHAN VS. DAN

Masquerade was able to get Chan Lee, the third-ranked brawler in the world, to join his side. When Chan Lee challenged Dan and his friends, Dan insisted on brawling her by himself.

Dan quickly saw why Chan Lee was such a highly ranked player. A master of strategy, she sent two of Dan's Bakugan to the Doom Dimension. Dan and Drago fought hard to defeat Chan Lee in the end. But for most of the battle, her Pyrus Fortress dominated the field.

Move 1

Dan has taken out two of Chan Lee's Bakugan. He throws down his Pyrus Mantris, planning to take down her last Bakugan and win the battle.

330

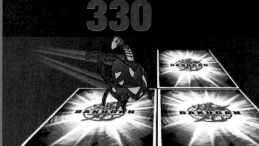

Move 2

Chan Lee's Pyrus Fortress takes the field with 370 Gs and stands on the card with Mantris. It's time to brawl! Dan starts to use an Ability Card to give Mantris extra power—but Chan Lee stops him.

330

370

Move 3

Chan Lee uses an Ability Card called Face of Greed. It cancels out the effects of Dan's Ability Card. Dan can't give Mantris the boost it needs. Fortress wins the round.

330

370

Move 4

Chan Lee brings out a special Ability Card that she can use after a battle. The card Revive brings her two lost Bakugan back into her arsenal. She's back on top!

DUEL IN THE DESERT

Dan and his friends took a trip to see Julie, who lives near Bakugan Valley. They were all searching the desert for the Infinity Core when two brawlers challenged them. One was Komba, a top-ranked champion, and the other was Billy, Julie's old friend.

Everyone was shocked to learn that Komba and Billy were fighting with Masquerade. Shun and Julie teamed up to beat the treacherous team. They won in the end—but Komba and Billy put up a tough fight.

Move 1

Komba tosses his Ventus El Condor onto a Gate Card.

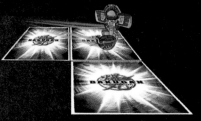

340

Move 2

Julie has a plan. She throws her Subterra Tuskor onto the Gate Card next to El Condor. Then she uses an Ability Card, Nose Slap. The card allows her to attack the Bakugan on a card touching hers. Since Tuskor has more Gs than El Condor, Julie thinks she's won the round.

350 340

Move 3

Komba uses an Ability Card, Blow Away, to stop Tuskor's attack. Then El Condor moves onto Tuskor's Gate Card.

350 340

Move 4

El Condor still doesn't have enough G's to take down Tuskor, but Komba has another move planned. He turns over the Gate Card, and El Condor gets a 100-G power boost. El Condor wins the round.

350 440

THE FINAL SHOWDOWN?

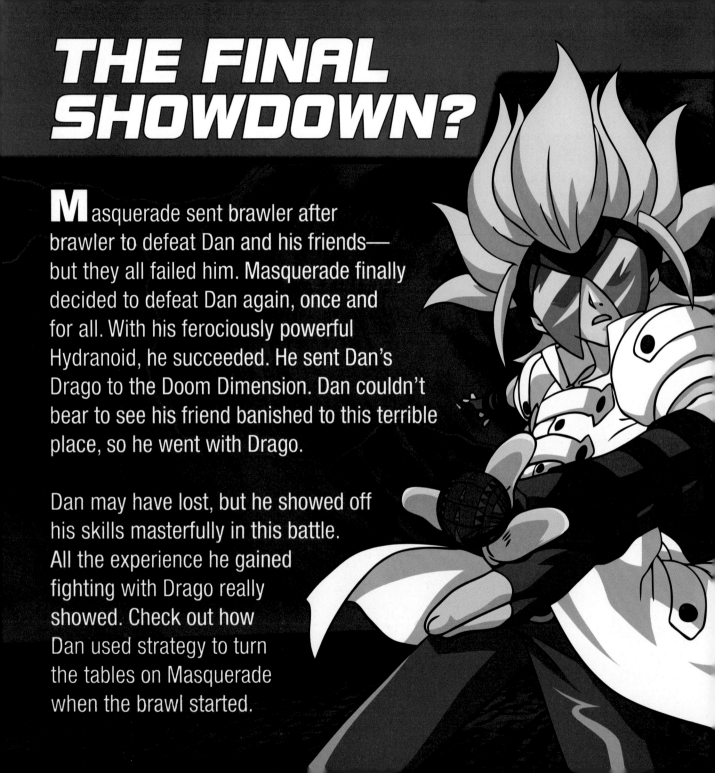

Masquerade sent brawler after brawler to defeat Dan and his friends— but they all failed him. Masquerade finally decided to defeat Dan again, once and for all. With his ferociously powerful Hydranoid, he succeeded. He sent Dan's Drago to the Doom Dimension. Dan couldn't bear to see his friend banished to this terrible place, so he went with Drago.

Dan may have lost, but he showed off his skills masterfully in this battle. All the experience he gained fighting with Drago really showed. Check out how Dan used strategy to turn the tables on Masquerade when the brawl started.

Move 1

After the first two Gate Cards are on the field, Masquerade throws out one more Gate Card. Then he tosses out Darkus Wormquake to stand on a card.

380

Move 2

Dan is eager to battle. He throws out his Pyrus Griffon, which has a 10 G advantage over Wormquake.

390

380

Move 3

Masquerade opens the Gate Card: Energy Merge. It takes away 100 Gs from Griffon and transfers them to Wormquake. Wormquake gets ready to take down Griffon.

290

480

Move 4

Dan counters with an Ability Card: Fire Tornado. It allows his Pyrus Bakugan to steal 100 Gs from its opponent. Now the tables have turned. Griffon has the most Gs, and Wormquake loses the round.

390

380

RUNNER-UP BATTLES

Dan and his friends have had many exciting battles—and they've only just begun to explore the game of Bakugan. Here are a few other great battle moments. Which one is your favorite?

The first time Dan and Runo teamed up in a brawl, they faced off against magicians Kenta and Kenji. This was the first time Drago and Tigrerra teamed up, too. They defeated Kenta and Kenji, sending a message to Masquerade—Dan and his friends would be tough to beat.

When Marucho and Runo went to visit Shun, he made a deal: If they could beat him, he would join them. Marucho and Runo tried, but Shun used some amazing moves to jack up his Skyress's power to 920 Gs! Marucho and Runo had never seen power like that before, and lost the battle.

After Billy was under Masquerade's control, he battled Julie again. Julie lost, and her Gorem was about to go to the Doom Dimension. Julie pleaded with her childhood friend, and something changed inside Billy. He took back the Doom Card and saved Gorem at the last second.